PATRICIA LILLIE

Jake and Rosie

 Greenwillow Books, New York

To my grandparents

Watercolor paints and colored pens
were used for the full-color art.
The text type is ITC Symbol.

Printed in Singapore by Tien Wah Press

First Edition
10 9 8 7 6 5 4 3 2 1

Library of Congress
Cataloging-in-Publication Data

Lillie, Patricia.
Jake and Rosie.
Summary: Jake is upset not to
find his best friend Rosie at
home, but Rosie soon returns
and shows Jake a nice surprise.
[1. Friendship — Fiction]
I. Title.
PZ7.L632Jak   1989
[E]   87-14939
ISBN 0-688-07624-6
ISBN 0-688-07625-4 (lib. bdg.)

Jake and Rosie were neighbors.
They were exactly the same size and their hair
was almost the same color.

They were best friends and did everything together.

One day, they decided to be twins.

They both put on blue jeans and red shirts.
Their shoes didn't match, so they traded
left shoes. That looked silly.
''You two giggle too much,'' said Rosie's
brother Peter.

They got out Rosie's crayons and drew
monsters. All the monsters were named
Peter, and that made them giggle even more.

Another day they decided to be pirates.
"You two should be locked up!" said Jake's sister.

So they built a jail and banged on the bars
and shouted "Let us go!" until it was time
for Rosie to go home for dinner.

They even had chicken pox at the same time.
They called each other on the telephone and said,
''Cock-a-doodle-doo! There's a pox all over you!''

One morning, after their poxes were all gone, Jake knocked on Rosie's door. But nobody answered. He tried to look in the windows. Rosie's house was dark and her car was gone.

Jake sat down to wait for Rosie. He waited for a long time, but she didn't come home. He shut his eyes and counted as high as he could, but when he opened his eyes — still no Rosie.

Jake climbed his favorite tree.
But Rosie still didn't come home.

"Jake! Where are you?" somebody hollered.
But it wasn't Rosie. It was just his sister.

Jake went to dig in the sandbox.
Rosie still didn't come home.

Then Jake saw somebody coming up the sidewalk!
But it wasn't Rosie. It was only the mailman.

Rosie's cat came to keep Jake company.

"Maybe Rosie's never coming back,"
Jake said.
But Pumpkinseed just curled up in a
ball and went to sleep.

Jake began to cry.

Jake's mother heard him.
"What's wrong, Jake?" she asked.

"Rosie's gone and I can't find her anywhere,"
   Jake said.
"Oh dear," Jake's mother said. "Are you
   sure?"

Then they heard a car.

"Where were you?" Jake shouted. "I thought you were never coming back!"

"We went shopping," Rosie said. "Look!"

And on her feet were new shoes,
just like Jake's.